THE Loss OF A SON

THE *Loss* OF A SON

A Journey Through Grief

GRANT CROSS

Primix Publishing
11620 Wilshire Blvd
Suite 900, West Wilshire Center, Los Angeles, CA, 90025
www.primixpublishing.com
Phone: 1-800-538-5788

Published by Primix Publishing: 09/19/2023

ISBN: 979-8-89194-003-1(sc)
ISBN: 979-8-89194-004-8(e)

Library of Congress Control Number: 2023916715

Contents

Introduction

Someone close maybe a family member, a friend, child, wife, husband or someone you may know is going through losing a loved one. This is a journey that I have experienced and I wish to share, to help others by telling my story on coping, getting through the darkness that seems to be all around me at the time, called death. My prayer is that you will gleam from this book that is being shared, and in some way be a practical guide for you to share with others or just for personal use. As with many things in life there is a choice in everything we do. I had to choose a thankful heart even when it seems everything was changing, the love of a loved one was slipping out of my hands and there was nothing I could do. I was in despair, but in the midst of it I knew life would get better. No matter how low or dark life may get there is always a light at the end of the tunnel.

My desire is that as you read this book, may it have an impact on your life so that you will be able to share it with those who are in pain right now, or someone that needs encouragement not to give up. There is a way through your darkness.

My prayer is that you will be moved enough to not just read this book but to put into practice what you learn while on your own journey.

This book is not about religion, yet I would not be able to tell the story if we left out the most important part of how Grant was able to get through those tough times. Scripture is quoted in this book. Without

Grant knowing Jesus and having a personal relationship with Him, it could have been a different outcome. After all, he knows about grief and sorrow as he experienced himself the day upon the cross when he called out to his father. "My God, My God, why have you forsaken me?" So for anyone who doesn't know Jesus as there Saviour, turn to the back of this book if you would like to know Him.

I have written a simple prayer for you to say and may you experience the freedom Grant did even while going through tragedy, for Jesus will never forsake you, just keep your eyes on Him for he is the way the truth and life everlasting. Always remember God made us. Take a look inside and see the person you were created to be.

So if you're keen, let's go and start the journey so grab a drink, put your feet up and let's get closer to our Jesus. After all, that is why He paid the price. There is no intention to convert you, just be open and you too will find Jesus real and will live a more purpose filled, peaceful, powerful, fulfilled life.

In this story, Damion Grant's son is referred to as Dame.

Chapter 1

It was a good day, first time Grant's boy had gone away except on school trips: this time he was going for sport, and although there was uneasiness in the inner parts of his heart, he let his son go! He still remembers that day as it was yesterday. Standing at the back door in the porch waving "see you Monday", watching as Dame and other boys from his surf boat crew got in one of the boy's car and left. Never for one moment thinking that would not see Dame alive again.

Grant felt he was truly bullet proof. He had a good life, good job, a loving wife (who he calls Col), four beautiful children, two boys and two girls, and yeah, life was good. So he thought because it was good in his eyes, (to be honest that was his gauge on how life was) he didn't realize his life was about to be turned upside down. There, in his own eyes, there was no need for change.

A couple of years ago Grant found peace that was new to him - he found Jesus.

Odd for this to happen to a man like him, as his lifestyle was not anywhere near to what religion or being a Christian seemed to him and his friends. He would do and say some really foolish things.

It was like he was on a mission to alienate those close to him, the ones he loved the most, his dearest friends ---*1 Cor 1:27 (KJV) "But God hath chosen the foolish things of the world to confound the wise; and God hath chosen the weak things of the world to confound the things which are mighty";* as many people do Grant had a preconceived idea of what it is to be a Christian knowing Jesus. The whole experience of meeting Jesus was not what he expected. How wrong his preconception had been. As Grant found Jesus was not there if he did good, if he lived as man said he should. This came as a surprise to him. In his younger years, he had been taught that there were certain things or ways to find God. This thankfully was not the case of his life. He found Jesus to be alive and actually care about everything he did including all his concerns, fears, weaknesses and all he had to do was give it all to him.

He could have saved many others in pain if he had been able to share that love if he had only realized how much love God had for him.

His journey started when Grant and Col decided to go to a weekend business trip. They hired a van and picked up some people they were in business with and headed on their way. It was about eight hours drive to get to their destination. Once there, they had a good couple of days. He decided he would check out this event called a non-denominational meeting before heading home. This better not be a church meeting he thought, as he drove to this event. When they arrived, music was playing. It was not a normal church music. The building was like a convention centre and nothing like a church. This was all new for Grant and he felt very uneasy at first. As he looked around the room they entered, he could not see any priest type person. This was a huge relief. They found a seat where escape was easy. In a row where there was nobody between them and the aisle.

"If I need to get out of here in a hurry I can" he thought. Yet there was a part of Grant that longed for more. From deep within, he needed change, maybe he would find what he had been looking for!

Then the music stopped and some man from Australia began to speak. He could relate to what was shared, in fact it seemed like the man was talking directly to him. No, how could this stranger know where his life was at. Then this man puts out an invitation for all those who want to know Jesus to put their hand up, Grant's hand went up, then it started… It felt like his heart was going to pump right out of his chest. He began saying to Col "look my hand went up, did you see that my hand went up." Col just looked at him as if to say yeah whatever. The man talking was oblivious to all that was happening to Grant. All of his life he thought he is in control of his life! This was not in his plan and he felt uneasy. Yet peace surrounded him. Then came an invitation to come up the front. "There's no way I'm going up to the front." Grant thought, remembering he was not usually seen anywhere near anything to do with church or God. And yet up the front he found himself amongst people in all different races from all parts of the world, all areas of society. There seemed to be no discrimination.

It was good. There was real peace. He was not concerned about his reputation, whether he had annoyed his wife or the others waiting for him. This was a new experience. It was better and peaceful. Had Grant taken a step in the right direction? Little did he know how much that one decision would help him through the storms of life that lay ahead in his life!

For the first time in his life, Grant felt real good. This Jesus was nothing like the picture he had in his belief system. Slowly change started to occur. He didn't feel any different but he no longer swore, he didn't drink and yeah life was good. When visitors and friends came to his house they made a comment on how peaceful and relaxed they felt. His house (body) was clean for the first time and in a long time, peace flowed through him touching many people he came in contact with.

However Grant began to wonder what would happen if he had a little drink or a smoke, maybe even just a little cone (marijuana)… so you guessed it… a little drink turned into 195% of where his drinking used to be, same for smoking and the cone. Grant now found himself in a worse place then before he stopped.

2Peter 2:22: "A dog goes back to its vomit," and "A sow that has been washed goes back to roll around in the mud

Mat 12:43 "When the unclean spirit has gone out of a man, he walks through dry places seeking rest, and finds none. Then he said, I will return into my house from where I came out. And when he has come, he finds it empty, swept, and decorated. Then he goes and takes with him seven other spirits more evil than himself, and they enter in and live there. And the last state of that man is worse than the first. Even so it also shall be to this evil generation."

Grant did not realize that the change he was experiencing in his life had been grace and mercy. He was not one of the people changed in an instant. He learned it was up to him and no one else would or could make the choices and decisions but only himself! This was not an easy thing to come to terms with for him as he had never known delayed gratification. Anything and everything he had wanted, he found a way and always get what he wanted. He thought he needed all he had gotten. Grant was oblivious to the damage. Like a marriage being blown apart, friendships being torn at the very root, employers running out of options to remain employed, such is not a very rosy picture.

The thing Grant found odd was that no matter what he did or where he went he could feel Jesus presence, like arms outstretched and waiting for his decision. He would go more intensely, at whatever he was into at that moment, until he lost control.

When he woke up one day, he knew all he had to do was surrender. How could this be? "Probably my imagination" he thought as he began thinking and recalling all that had happened before he slept, he cringed. Sadly he never understood it was his choice for many years. He did not understand that a lot of people were watching him, why, who knows, (maybe they were seeking something real or someone to fill the emptiness inside them.) Maybe they had been involved or someone close, a friend, family in some religion that lead them further away from freedom. Anyway they were watching. He was slipping back to his old ways, when he drank he knew it was wrong yet he kept on drinking and really not being concerned about anyone, or anything. The Apostle Paul talks about this in

Rom 7:19 "For the good which I have a mind to do, I do not: but the evil which I have no mind to do, that I do".

This was not how Grant desired to be, he often dreamed of being a better person. Someone who brings joy and peace to the atmosphere, not fear anger, confusion and disruption. He knew in his heart there was more and he longed not to do the random things, of which often hurt the people closest to him. Many times he would set out to do something, go somewhere not a thought entered his mind regarding drinking or any other activity that would transform him, into someone focused at the moment, and all that was in that moment with him. It was a very lonely place to be, often he would think if only I could be the person I know is inside. Every time he thought that way, the thought seemed to vanish before it had any chance of becoming reality. Like a child, if things didn't go his way he threw everything out the cot. Like driving a car, life is full of choices; Grant thought knowing Jesus was doing the same things, drinking, drugs, womanizing, anger, selfishness and much more.

And Jesus changed all that needed changing, this is not how Jesus works. He had to make the right choices and then implement that choice in his life even though he was living on a dead end and he knew it. He needed to learn even if Jesus wasn't cheering him on and the choices he was making were keeping him away from Jesus. If he turned his life around made different choices he would find Jesus waiting arms outstretched. Grant was a little gun shy of religion as he thought well he was not sure what he thought. No matter what he did all that seemed to give him peace was when he turned back to Jesus!

As time went on he began to coach sweep (the sweep stands at the rear steers of the surfboat) a surfboat crew and Grant enjoyed this, for he liked the sea and had spent a lot of time on the sea. There was nothing else he had found that gave him such a natural high. The sea is a powerful opponent. There were times when it felt that it was like he was being watched over. From a young age certain things happened with outcomes that where unreal.

Like the time when he had been surfing on his new surfboard, first time in the water, nice waves, and good weather. Grant had caught and rode a nice wave, came off the wave all good. He started to paddle out behind the breakers, he dove under the first wave come up and there: heading straight for him was a four man surf canoe. Not more than twenty metres away on a big wave going fast, Grant knew he had to do something fast so he dived down leaving his new board to its fate. When he come to the surface there was his new board nearly cut in half. There had been another time when Grant was out with his mates, having fun as young people do: not realizing at any time the danger he was in as they spent along a country road, a rock wall on one side, and a 300 meter drop on the other side. As we approached the left hand bend, the driver lost control and as the car slid toward the side of the metal road, the momentum had taken the car away from the sheer drop and the car ended up in a fence. Three metres away from the drop that would have… well let's just say we were glad it didn't happen.

As Grant become older there were many more times that things happened in which the outcome did not seem right for the situation. Like the time he was driving a half full LPG tanker, this was a big unit 500 horsepower Mack truck with a semi-trailer, driving on country roads. Although they were main roads they are still not very wide. On the edge of the road is the water table, sometimes the angle is steep and sometimes it's not. (In this part of the road it was very steep.)

As he rounded a corner onto a bridge the road was straight before him, he reached down for a smoke, when he looked up his truck was on the shoulder, which was very steep this combined with tanker being half full of LPG, caused it to start to roll. He changed half a gear, aimed for the centre line and put his foot down, there was no traffic coming and he could see up the road a few hundred metres. The whole unit was swaying violently from side to side, Grant was thankful he was wearing his seat belt, and the road was clear….

> *1Sa 22:23 "Keep here with me and have no fear; for he who has designs on my life has designs on yours: but with me you will be safe."*

He got to his next stop and looked at the tyres on the trailer and could see marks up the side of the tyres 150 to 200 millimetres: the truck should have rolled over.

In his teenage years he was working in roofing. One job he was on, replacing guttering on a big building, which was used for bus maintenance and repair. The job was to remove the gutter, and replace it. All the bottom screws had to be removed. So away they went, doing what had to be done. Grant was thinking to himself sweet easy job: Then came the other side. Because these sheets were short, and only had two rows of screws to get the gutter out both rows of screws had to be taken out. About half way through, this part of the job, the other man who was the senior had to go and pick something up. Before leaving, he said to Grant "don't stand on the short sheets there is nothing holding them and you could fall". "All good" he said, and he got on with the job.

About ten minutes into pulling up the gutter Grant stood on the short sheet. Because he was facing the other way, it made the job easier. He thought to himself, "if the sheet slips I'll jump onto the other side. On he went everything was going well. Next moment he was falling. Now if he had fallen straight down, he would have landed, onto sheet metal. This sheet metal was standing up, on a lean, in racks, different gauge (thickness), about ten sheets, in each gauge, in each rack, there were around thirty racks. Grant would have been diced. Grant was real glad, that for some reason, he went sideways. Six or seven metres, landing in a roof truss. He was facing downward, when he saw a man looking at him, odd there is no pain, he thought, the man said "you ok mate hang on, help is coming to get you down." Grant was straddling the roof truss, still around 8 metres off the floor.

After they got Him down, they took him to their first aid room. Laying on the bed waiting for the ambulance, he started to think about what had just happened.

Then the ambulance arrived and in came two paramedics, now one was a new graduate.

When she saw the blood coming from Grant's wounds, (he had split his top lip, and his elbow had split open revealing the bone) she fainted. Everyone who had been attending to him went to help this young woman's aide. Leaving Grant alone watching as everyone there helped the young woman paramedic; he found this to be amusing helping him take his mind of his own injuries and pain. After this he was taken to hospital, stitched up sent home, after a few weeks rest he was back to full strength.

One day Grant was talking with his mother and she told him how when he was born, the doctor told her and his Dad that their baby probably wouldn't make it. Grant had been born weak, not breathing properly and something was wrong that the doctors were a bit puzzled and they had no answers. Yet he is still very much alive. There are many more instances when Grant should have been dead... was there a reason he never died!

Grant enjoyed life even though the peace and presence of his friend Jesus seemed to be getting more and more distant. He had no idea that Jesus actually hadn't gone anywhere; he was standing right beside him. It was only the choices he made, that kept Grant distant.

What lay ahead? If he had known; maybe things would have been different; (yeah) making better choices would have meant less pain! There were times when he wondered why he hurt the people he cared about, and hurt them he did. In fact, if there was an award for hurting people, he would have been a contender.

The people he would hurt, were not people that just liked him, oh no, they were family and those close to Grant. He knew in his heart what he was doing was wrong and yet try as he did, to stop hurting them, he would he just kept on doing the same things

Rom 7:19 "For the good which I have a mind to do, I do not: but the evil which I have no mind to do, that I do."

Grant could see good friends distancing themselves. Any time there was a party or barbeque, or some form of gathering he would not be invited. Not because he was not liked but because he was out of control. Simple things like if someone looked at him the wrong way, he would want to fight them. (So furniture would get broken and sometimes people hurt, you get the picture)? He was fine when he wasn't under the influence of drink, sort of like a Jekyll and Hyde personality.

It was never his fault he would always blame someone else, even when he knew he was. This seemed to work, taking away any blame or responsibility, or so Grant thought. Unfortunately he found out, as happens in life, you reap what you sow.

Gal 6:7 "Do not be deceived, God is not mocked. For whatever a man sows, that he also will reap."

Pro 22:8 "He who sows iniquity shall reap vanity; and the rod of his anger shall fail."

Grant had, caused havoc and destruction in his life which were about to catch up to him. He did not know this? If he had, there would have been things done differently. He was not aware that most of the seed he'd sown. He was going to reap not a good harvest could have been removed, cut of, pulled out. There would have been consequences nothing like what was heading his way, like an out of control freight train.

Act 3:19 "Therefore repent and convert so that your sins may be blotted out, when the times of refreshing shall come from the presence of the Lord."

Many times Grant would be told you're just thinking of yourself and have no regard for anyone but yourself. When told this he brushed it of as whoever told him, has the problem, after all how could it be him. Yes he was in deception.

2Ti 3:2-4 "For men will be self-lovers, money- lovers, boasters, proud, blasphemers, disobedient to parents, unthankful, unholy, without natural affection, unyielding, false accusers, without self- control, savage, despisers of good, traitors, reckless, puffed up, lovers of pleasure rather than lovers of God."

It was not until many years and much, so much, pain later that he understood what that meant! In the meantime he kept on living life according to his rules. This meant if things were going his way it was all good, if not, look out-- anger would be unleashed, words would be spoken, words that, meant to hurt, and cut to the soul as they were spoken. He would do this mostly because he wanted to win, not realising how cruel, and devastating the words he was speaking were; to others and himself. He had a real mean streak. Then Grant would wonder why people were upset – and he would say things like "What's up"? "Why have thrown your toys out"?" You really need to sort yourself out".

Now at the time it never occurred to him that he was the one with the problem, was he short sighted? Who knows? Now because he didn't see himself as the one causing these storms, he carried on doing the same things, then wondering why his friends were a little distant.

Not only his friends but also Col and his family (we hurt the ones closest to us the most) try as he might, he could not stop this. But it all caught up with him in the long run.

He had a good real good friend, his name was Stretch. When Stretch and Grant were younger they, got a pin and pricked their fingers and became blood brothers, they were good mates. However he pushed their friendship to the edge. This happened so often as they grew up until one day their relationship changed, and they became just friends. As they continued to grow apart, he never realized anything was wrong until it was too late: It seemed every time Grant tried to do good, it seemed to turn out wrong.

Now he did love his family and tried his hardest to provide all they needed, unfortunately for Grant he had more to learn. He knew there was more to life, he had an inner desire to do better and be better, and he just tried all the wrong ways. He had heard "it's the little things that matter" and thought how true I must remember that and put it into action he never did!

Chapter 2

It was a good day, first time his boy Dame had gone away except on school trips: this time he was going for sports, and although there was uneasiness in the inner parts of Grant's heart, he let his son go. The relationship he had with Dame was awesome, they were like best mates, and they had their moments. Usually initiated by Grant's stubbornness. Try as he would he could not get the uneasiness he felt to go away. So he did what he knew would take away anything, he got wasted, stoned, yeah now it was all good or so he thought. Time for bed he had no trouble getting to sleep, any wonder.

Then he was awake someone was at the gate trying to get in (the gate was padlocked to keep the dog in) the dog was barking. So out of bed Grant got, thinking it was some drunk at the wrong house, it was the police. And that gut feeling came back… what are the police doing here in middle of the night?

Funny thing is, he already knew in his heart why: There had been an accident their Dame was in a bad way… He was awake, wide awake, is he alive? How bad is Dame hurt?

Grant's head began to spin; Col began to cry he went back in time to when Dame had asked if he could go, the uneasiness he had felt ignored said ok. That was when the guilt started he blamed himself from that moment with all the other emotions always on top was guilt. Grant, Col, the police officer had all gone upstairs and where in the kitchen. He asked the police woman What about the other boys in the car? What a job; you hear about the darker side of police work, most people never get to experience or see it thankfully. They were told two of the boys were dead. Grant's heart missed a beat; please God let this be a dream. It is truly amazing how in times of troubled waters, we turn to God even when God is not part of their life.

Could this be because we really want to go to someone who understands, who knows their every need how much they hurt, in pain we can look and see someone in pain through injury, this could be from playing sport, a work related injury, anything external that can be seen. If the Pain is not from external injury we may see the pain and not recognize the suffering or know the circumstances.

So most people turn and walk away, so we turn to God even when we don't know who God is what he stands for, what he expects or wants from us we turn to God. Often the information we have concerning God comes distorted, and has heaps of rules, dos and don'ts. In a time when all else brings no respite from the pain, cry out to God get to know Jesus.

Was their Dame dead? No! He was in the hospital. Relief and hope began to arise in Grant. He really wanted Dame to be ok and to be able to return home and carry on with his life.

Where the car had crashed was in a gorge, far away from any hospital, Dame's foot was stuck under the front seat, when they got his foot free, it was too windy to lift him out by the rescue chopper. So they had to carry him up a ten metre wall. All this took time unfortunately Dame couldn't afford any time delay. The pressure on his brain was doing major damage. He thought of his son frightened, alone in the dark with no noise except the river flowing, calling out to his mates but no answer!

The 10 meter fall would have been horrific for them, hearing the voices of his mates as fear ripped through the occupants in the car. Then silence! The unknown if only I had gone this thought followed him for a long time. Grant imagined Dames last moments; through the silence voices rescue was near. The boys from the other car standing up the top by the road unable to get down to the crashed car could hear

Dame calling "help me" they were the last words spoken by his son before he lost conciseness.

Grant was lost, thankfully his good friend Stretch, whose nephew was in the same car, had organized plane tickets for the parents to fly up to where the boys were. Upon arrival they were picked up and taken to the hospital. This was done when Stretch saw his own family in pain his mate who was like a dad to him dying of cancer this is true compassion putting aside your own feelings, pain to help and be there for others.

As Grant and Col walked toward the doors to Intensive care, he felt guilt that if he had of gone along, none of this would of happened. At the time this added pressure was hard so very hard to carry. This guilt was not only for his son, it was the three boys. All the fear all the pain the three boys suffered, and the parents, the families, so much so overwhelming. If he had of given all of his emotion, thoughts, feelings to Jesus he would have not had carry the guilt or any other emotion that was negative not uplifting towards his family or those around him. This is not to say it would be easy, that there would have been no pain no what he is saying is "it wouldn't have been as hard or lonely", For as the emotion came he could have given it to Jesus as the guilt came he could have given it to Jesus. The pain would have still been there and yes he would still have to walk through the grief; it would be with someone who knew what he was, feeling, thinking. You see as Grant eventually found out Jesus wants to help to walk with you through all things in life.

He was also these boys' coach (sweep stands on the back of the surf boat steers the boat motivates works at keeping control and order within the crew) and it was the only time he had not gone away with his son and crew (this gave access to more guilt, this guilt is a waste of energy, can lead to depression, bad decision making, this can lead to a whole lot more pain regret and sorrow):

The doors to the Intensive care were locked, you had to speak into a speaker to tell the nurses inside who you are and why you wanted to enter. After what seemed like an eternity the doors opened, while he waited his mind went into overdrive.

What is Dame like? I've been told "he looks fine" maybe he's having some sort of seizer this went on and on in his mind until the doors opened. They were directed toward their son's bed, relief he looked fine (as is said looks can be deceiving) there was a bandage on his head no major wounds. That was until the nurse came, and told them both about the pressure on his brain. Would he make it through? Was the first question asked, a doctor would be here and explain more? So they waited while Dame was in an induced coma. He couldn't talk so they both talked to him and held his hand. What do you do when one of your children lay there helpless? You try to be up for their sake. Talking, believing they will be ok, trying to comfort them the best way you can. Nothing could have prepared Grant for what laid ahead...

The doctor came and explained all about pressure on the brain. That it had been caused, by blunt force trauma to the head. It affected the basic functioning of Dame's body, basically the motor function which among lots of other areas, enables breathing, and even if he pulled through, the chance of major brain damage was high. It was good to know all about Dame's condition to be given some explanation to what is going on. Although to be honest the information went over his head everything spoken all noise was muffled to him he could sort of hear what was being said, it just didn't seem to register.

At some stage when the car went over the edge, Dame sustained a blow to the top of his head, this caused pressure on his brain. In reality it is hard to take in as you are in a state of unbelief or shock. So although you hear what is being said it has to be replayed in your mind over and over, before it was understood. Because in intensive care they were very busy, the doctor was called away leaving Grant and Col a little more informed. Really all that they both wanted was for Dame to be ok and go home with them. All he desired or longed for was to have Dame back take him home to hear his voice hold him close, he never knew this wasn't going to happen!

Then there was a lot of activity around Dame, trying not to get in the way, he found out Dame was being moved by chopper to Starship Hospital (children's hospital in Auckland, New Zealand) as he was fourteen nearly fifteen. They looked at one another; the atmosphere was electric between Col and Grant. Who should go in the helicopter? There is only one spare seat, so who goes and who drives?

They both wanted to go with Dame, and yet they wanted to stay together, this was the first decision they had to make while in a state of shock, turmoil, unbelief. The outcome, a car was hired, and they drove the two hours to Starship Children's Hospital. There was not a lot said throughout the drive he was just numb, the song I will always love you, (by Whitney Houston) kept playing over and over in his mind. The guilt was never far away so all-consuming, such a waste of thought, energy. The word of God says "Stay strong cast out of your mind anything negative".

This is not easy especially with everything else unfolding before him at this time. (There will be people that need you at your best. Always try to focus on the future it will keep coming: be strong.) Grant and Col did not know what lay ahead! As they walked through Starship Hospital they saw all races, all, types of people from all different parts of society: with one thing in common a child suffering, illness, pain. On they walked, toward intensive care, where Dame was. He had never felt anything like what he was feeling an apprehension, fear of the unknown. He had that same feeling; when Dame first went away, deep in his heart; try as he did he could not stop the felling: It was like he knew things were not going to turn out well... He didn't want to think negatively he tried oh how he tried to keep positive keep thinking Dame would be ok, however the feeling of pending disaster of loss was never far away.

As they arrived at the reception of intensive care, they told the lady there who they were. They were shown into a waiting room, having been told Dame was in surgery, the doctors were trying to relieve the pressure on his brain. After what seemed like hours, but in reality was only about twenty minutes. Grant and Col were taken to Dame, he looked so peaceful, like he had just finished playing rugby had a knock to the head, (Dame had a bandage on his head) had a shower, and was having a sleep, there was nothing wrong; Oh how wrong that picture was. Dame was in an induced coma. So Grant and Col sat beside Dame's bed, hoping... believing the best, soon Dame would wake up say "hi": After sitting with Dame they both looked up. There was a woman standing at the end of Dame's bed, she took Grant and Col to a room, where she identified herself, as Caroline doctor in charge of intensive care.

Grant had been hit, in his stomach before; he had even been kicked in the stomach. When the doctor told Grant and Col they could not release the pressure on Dame's brain, he wasn't going to make it. That was like something reached in grabbed his heart, stood on it, twisted it, his heart missed a beat. Holding Col close Grant could hear the sobbing, feel her body trembling.

If only you had gone none of this would have happened it was never ending over and over in his mind. As a parent he had made right and wrong choices with Dame, oh how he loved his son so much what now?

Is this real I must be dreaming, please God let this be dream. Grant was brought back to reality by the doctor. She told them after 24 hours they will run a series of tests then if there is no response they turn of Dame's life support. His emotions were out of control he didn't know what to do what was going to happen at this moment all that consumed him was loss pain and sorrow. He would like to be able to say he looked to Jesus took all his emotions, loss pain; the truth is at this time he never. Thankfully Jesus had not left him and helped him and his family through all before them.

Caroline then explained after they had some time alone together, for them both to spend as much time as they can with Dame, staying positive around him. When you have a loved one in a life or death situation it is not an easy thing to hold them knowing in your heart this is the last few hours you may see them alive: Really all they wanted was to wake him and take Dame home!

The message given by the doctor was the exact opposite; as they got seated beside Dame Grant felt numb, empty, and useless. Hear lay his son, breathing only because of a ventilating machine. Once the ventilator is turned off, the chances of Dame breathing on his own were low, very low: Beside him, Col was holding Dames hand somewhere a piece of Grant began to die, the guilt, the shame of failing to protect his family firmly took up a piece of his mind. Although no one said anything concerning, guilt, shame, or anything to do with this, he felt everyone knew it was his fault. There was like a dark fog enveloping him, surrounding, consuming him. Try as he did he just couldn't get the all-consuming feeling of guilt, shame, and doom to leave. The only thing he had not done is entered into a time of prayer.

Because he felt so unworthy like why would God be interested in such a looser as me? This was so far from the truth God's love for him had never been any less; it was only the perception Grant had in his mind. How did he come to this way of thinking? It maybe had something to do with what was going on in his life! Or it could be a combination of both! Or was it because he was broken and all of the above weakened him to a point he believed negative thoughts any thoughts. So he blamed himself for all that had happened and his decision making became weak and obscure. It doesn't have to be this way!

In any time of trial when our mind turns to negative thinking, try even though it usually is not easy to move out from a place where there seems no exit. Grant knew he was on the wrong path, yet at this time he kept focusing on the negative in his own life. He would look at others their needs, even doing all he could making people around him to be comfortable. On the outside everything seemed as it should inside there was no peace.

Dame never moved, Dame just laid there, all through the night, Dame laid so peaceful. He loved Dame so much. Grant hurt so much, there is no way to explain the hurt, no words can express that moment, and at times it all just overcame him. So he got up found somewhere where he was alone, and broke, wept, sobbed. Then back to Dame's bedside, this is a very odd feeling he thought. Sitting here beside my son knowing, that in a few hours, Dame could well be gone from his life. "Now is not the time for those kind of thoughts" He told himself.

He got up and went to make Col and himself a hot drink, while doing this he began to think, of what he had herd been taught about these situations, all that he could believe was, he had failed big time, he was consumed by a sorrow, his mate, his son, his Dame, wasn't going to be there. And yet in all the darkness, there was a little light. He knew he wasn't alone, strange in this time of, brokenness, loss, grief, so many different emotions, feelings; someone was holding him and that was the strength that kept Grant going.

We are given grace and strength to enable us to get through tough situations in life as life is not always fair but it is always just, that is the way God is.

How can I feel so useless, like such a failure, so far away from God, and yet he knew there was a supernatural power, a love, a strength, In such at time as this. He had to be there for his family strong, everything that had happened to this point he could not change however he could change for the future! To be honest he had no idea how he this was going to work out. How do you change the future when life has been a struggle he resigned to do his best? Hot drinks in hand he headed back to Dame's bedside. Grant could sense the sadness the impending loss; maybe some of what he was encountering was coming from Dame. Col was doing a great job of masking her hurting, pain in front of Dame. When Col got up, he moved over took hold of Dame's hand held Dame's hand close to his heart, Grant began to pray, Lord God if Dame is not going to be whole take Dame home to be with you.

But Lord please renew him give back to us. As Grant prayed he could feel a love so strong, compassion unfortunately his belief was that Dame would be going home to be with Jesus.

Believing this was good, as it helped Grant get through a very rough time in his life. It also meant his belief was Dame was not going to be back made well returning home with them alive.

Mar 4:40 "And He said to them, Why are you so fearful? How is it that you have no faith?"

Joh 11:40 "Jesus answered her, Did I not say to you that if you would believe you would see the glory of God?" He would be home with Jesus; this is not a bad thing. We always like to think we are further or closer to God; Dame will be.

Jesus is close to us; waiting for the thinking to change to believing. Always remember God will never love you more than he does right now! Yes it is true; to experience our heavenly fathers love, when we seek him with all our heart with all our soul with our entire mind.

Now you could be thinking this God stuff is not for me it is not real! As Grant once did. Then he realized to walk a true walk with Jesus was better than any drugs any drinking yes and although walking with Jesus was awesome it was not easy. (Because he was trying to do things his way with a little help from Jesus, instead of the other way around) No matter how tuff or strong we are doing the right thing is not easy however it is worth it.

> *Mat 22:37-40 "Jesus said to him, You shall love the Lord your God with all your heart, and with all your soul, and with all your mind. This is the first and great commandment. And the second is like it, you shall love your neighbour as yourself. On these two commandments hang all the Law and the Prophets."*

This has been part of Grant's Life Journey a work in progress but that is another story. Soon enough it became light outside this brought the realisation the time was drawing near when the ventilator will be turned off. This started his mind racing what is going to happen now? How is everyone going to react when the ventilator is turned off?

Whether panic fear of the unknown, or whether it was the enormity of the tragedy unfolding, he was lost. He didn't know where to look what to say he just didn't know.

Thankfully, Col's sister, her partner, Col's Mum, Grant and Col's oldest daughter, had driven through the night and had arrived before anything was done to establish Dame's condition. If Dame breathes on his own that will be a sign that he will survive. As Caroline began the testing, Grant was alert listening, watching, and hoping for a sign of life hoping... His focus was on Dame and dame alone anything could have happened around him Grant was focused on his son looking hoping for a sign of life it never came.

Although they were in intensive care, and there was lots happening around them, when the time came to turn the ventilator off.

It became quite as everyone watched Dame's chest to see some movement any sign he could breath, there was none. Now this is not an easy situation for anyone to be in.

He would have much rather not been there with his son his wife daughter and other family members. Watching as his son's chest never raised by itself no life no not one bit. Knowing in his heart that life was never going to be the same, at least they all had the chance to say their goodbyes to Dame. This was not an easy time trying to stay positive while saying goodbye! How hard it must be when a loved one is just gone!

The ventilator was turned back on. It was only a matter of time now; he had an understanding of what would happen. There would be about 30 to 40 tests done if no life was found then, morphine would be given to Dame and then the ventilator would be turned off. The tests took a long time and when Caroline turned to Grant and Col, not a lot was said. The ventilator was turned off they all watched as Dames chest stopped moving, nothing changed in the way Dame looked. It was a lot quieter around Dame's bed with all the machines turned off. Grant could hear a faint sobbing, as he opened his eyes, they were shut, in all the grief, pain, emptiness, uncertainty, there was a kind of peace, having his eyes closed made it easier to be in that place of peace. It was like Grant was about to fall off a cliff into a deep canyon, when he looked down he couldn't see the bottom. There where arms holding Grant so strong, so much love, that seemed to be holding him. This was all very real unfolding before him. As everyone does he had choices he could have completely lost it, causing more pain to those already hurting. Oh how he wanted to break something cause someone to hurt like he hurt. Thankfully he knew not to. He could sense, feel through all the pain a love a peace he had never known before. It was not overpowering, more consuming taking hold of him in his time of need. He just knew a love so deep was with him at that time. There was understanding in the love like where it was coming from knew what was to come and how to get through it. This was comforting as he had no idea of what was about to happen.

There was Col, tears rolling down her face, holding Kelly there oldest daughter, tears flowing down her face, Col's sister and nana holding them both tears flowing down there face, as.

Grant turned back to Dame who was still, he just lay there like he was sleeping, so still, numbness came over him. It was so quiet... He heard like a big window shattering only it was in his mind! Instead of glass he could see particles flying around then nothing sobbing he was hurting he was hurting real bad. And then he was consumed by guilt for in his heart he believed none of this would have happened had he been there. Why he felt this way never understood for many years.

Grant had heard of people who had lost someone close, seen movies, even new people who had family or friends pass on. He even had lost good friends, and in his mind he was confident of his reaction: In any case what he thought and all confidents went somewhere, because at that moment, it felt like a dam had broken, kind of surreal. The tears that were flowing were big, (like you can have rain that is misty, you can have rain that is consistent, you can have rain with big rain drops) he felt like a river of sorrow was flowing from deep within.

Grant was brought back to reality by Caroline, explaining they were going to take all the tubes out of Dame clean him up. Please could Grant and his family give her and her team half an hour alone with Dame?

Grant, Col and their family left the room went out for a cigarette. As he sat down his eyes meet Col's in the eyes of his wife there was pain, loss, sorrow. Then his eyes looked upon his daughter in her eyes pain, loss, and confusion. As Kelly not only saw the pain in her mum dad and family, she was walking in her own grief. How what can I do? There in front of him he saw his family in such pain. All he wanted was for! The pain he saw his family going through to be gone. How when in his own heart the pain the emptiness, loss was all consuming. He had to try and get his thinking away from all that was happening around him. He thought "I know I will focus on others help them as best I can then my focus will be on others" he said, I won't have to deal with my pain till later. He found out that sort of thinking only works for a short time.

He found it is nice to think of others and focus on their needs it does help however he had to deal with what is happening in his own mind as well. There comes a time when everything must be dealt with to move on, the longer things are left the harder to deal with they become.

Grant had people he had to ring, they were waiting for news of Dames condition' hoping for a positive outcome. He began calling, as he began to talk, it hit him again tears began to fall, as he tried to be strong; it became impossible to talk.

Instead of making calls to all the people he made one call explained the situation and left the phone calls for the person he rang to make. At that time in his life he felt it necessary to be strong and steady for his family. He tried on the outside it looked like; he had it all together how could anyone really have it altogether? Even if someone's heart through the things life had brought their way has been hardened. What is being expressed may not always be accurately perceived by everyone (someone may say or do something that is not really what they meant to say or do). However in his life all the different experiences there are no words or way to explain how Grant felt at that moment.

It was time to go back in, Grant called out to Jesus as he walked what seemed like a never ending walk, he felt a peace rise up from the inside, and this peace enabled him to continue on. Be sure not read he called out Jesus and read on when he called it was more like a cry from his inner self the very heart of his soul he had nowhere to go didn't know what to say or do he needed Jesus. He needed help he needed the pain to go. When he called out he found a love so all- consuming, any time any place anyone can call out and get to know Jesus.

Even when the guilt he had felt earlier began to surround how mind; Even though he had decided to focus on others not himself helping others where and when and how he could.

Grant didn't realize all he was doing was suppressing his own grief and everything was getting bottled up inside. The only thing that really helped amongst the grief, loss was the warmth deep inside. In reality the warmth, love so strong was keeping all the suppressed emotion from blowing in his life.

As Grant walked back into the ward where Dame lay so still so peaceful, All The tubes where gone, the machines all gone and Dame he loved so much was gone. All that was left lying before him was flesh the body Dames body his son gone! Grant believed with all his heart Dame was in a better place, and yet the pain was all consuming.

> *Ps 20:6 "Now I know that Jehovah saves His anointed;*
> *He will hear him from His holy Heaven with the saving*
> *strengths of His right hand"*

Grant's body felt numb, yet it hurt every part of his body was sore, Grant's mind was out of control, grief to grieve an emotion something he thought he could handle how wrong he had been.

Our mind how powerful, even to the point of you believing something we have no understanding of have never been through. And still we will give advice to others well-meaning of course, when we know absolutely nothing of what we are talking about. Grant was a mess still some of his emotion his feelings he did his best to supress. He had to stay strong for his family!

Grant sat down beside Dame the sound of sobbing filled the room, sorrow, loss, unbelief. He knew Dame was gone, yet as his gaze went to Dame, he looked so peaceful. As he reached for Dames hand his eyes meet Col's. There was nothing but sadness. It was hard enough for himself, at that moment he realized. How hard this must be on Col, as she had carried Dame for nine months, gave birth to Dame, whenever Dame was sick he would go straight to Col. Although broken hearted, he began to think of all the people, affected by this tragedy. For there were too other boys families, that never had chance to say goodbye.

How hard would that be? (There are so many times in this world when a loved one walks out the door, gets into a vehicle, boards a plane…, is gone never to return. All that is left, unbelief, hurt and pain, sorrow, how hard would that be not being able to say goodbye, tell them how much they were loved.)

Grant was deep in thought as waves of sorrow washed over him; you could say he was reflecting what if he had of stopped Dame from going? What if he had taken the time off work and gone with Dame and the other boys? What if what if what if at the end of the day Dame was gone from this world and in a better place? Really the what if sort of thinking doesn't help as he found out all it does is hold you from moving forward and on with life. He had a peace, amongst all the torment there was peace, like he was being comforted, still the pain was there and ooh how it hurt, he somehow had to snap out of this place. After all he had the rest of his family to think of. This in itself was no easy task when he was wallowing in a very low place himself! He knew he had to rise above all that had happened he did not know how to do this! There in this time of loss was it ok to be a little down a little lost still he felt he had to be strong for his family and the people affected by this tragic loss. As soon as he began thinking this way he felt better however all he was doing suppressing emotions and things that needed to be faced and dealt with.

Grant thought about times when he would be out doing whatever it be drinking, smoking (getting stoned). He never gave a second thought to his family, maybe because he knew they were safe? Now all he seemed to be thinking about was his family how he could support them be strong in there time of need. Always the thought none of this would have happened had you gone, would return consuming his mind overtaking his life.

Caroline told them both to go have cuppa, away from the hospital, as it would be hard, traumatic to be here when the undertakers came. Grant, Col and the rest of the family left. As Grant got up from Dame's bedside his eyes meet other parents in the ward. Although nothing was said; he felt their compassion. Yet you could sense a fear, apprehension, what lay ahead in their lives. Others were thankful they would not be walking this path. He continued to walk choosing not to look into eyes of any of people he walked past; He was consumed by the loss. He had no idea what to do or say really he wasn't concerned he needed to get some air everything was beginning to get on top of him. Still he could feel compassion and understanding holding him together not overpowering just there.

As Grant sat down he realized people were waiting to hear how Dame was doing, this meant he would have to ring: He took his phone out of his pocket and sat there staring, not knowing what to say, wondering if he would be able to say anything: As he rang the first person he felt another wave of grief, sadness begin to wash over him. The phone call was short and to the point. All the other calls well they were condensed into one and that took every bit of composer hr had left within him.

How do you tell someone anyone that your son has passed never to be seen again on earth?

Chapter 3

Grant, Col and their family started walking to Ronald McDonald house (Ronald McDonald house is a charitable house for people to stay when a loved one is in hospital in a time of need) where they were shown to their rooms, and all other conveniences they would need. The person they were dealing with who had shown them around absolutely awesome. They made the whole family feel at home. Very special people bless them all Lord God Jehovah.

Grant went out to get a coffee spend a bit of time on his own. After making his coffee he went out onto the deck sitting down at a big round table, he did not notice there was a lady sitting on the other side of the table. As his gaze lifted he noticed her. "Hi I'm Aroha sorry to hear about your son" she said "thank you" he replied. As they began to talk he learned Aroha was at Starship with her son who was battling leukaemia. She had already lost one son and her husband to leukaemia.

Any self-pity Grant felt, all sorrow, left for a moment as before him sat a lady who should have been bitter, angry and so much more was full of life optimism, strength, compassion. It is strange in the moment Grant was at the lowest point, thinking how could life be worse! There in front of him was Aroha so full of life she had learnt a valuable lesson, to be thankful, be an overcomer. As Aroha got up to go to her son's bedside he was filled with strength, a peace as he had never experienced before.

2Co 12:9 "And He said to me, My grace is sufficient for you, for My power is made perfect in weakness. Most gladly therefore I will rather glory in my weaknesses, that the power of Christ may overshadow me".

Joh 14:27 "Peace I leave with you, My peace I give to you. Not as the world gives do I give to you. Let not your heart be troubled, neither let it be afraid"

Grant had no understanding of what was happening to him at this time: all he knew was, it gave him strength to carry on, the pain eased.

Even though it was for a short time he knew he had been recharged from the inside out. He felt he was able to be there for his family. He can't explain why or how he knew in his heart he was going to make it through. He was brought back from his thoughts by Col and the family that were there, sitting at the table. It was a blessing that some of their family were there with them and could stay for one night. The other two had families they could stay with. There seemed to be an atmosphere of unbelief every time Grant would see Kelly; he expected to see Dame not far behind her, it wouldn't happen, these are the little things that take a long time to overcome. Grant tried to keep himself busy with what? Not much to do here! Ok let's have a rest of course you can't sleep, his mind started. At first there were good memories of Dame at rugby, the talks he would have with Dame how Dame would listen like a good son then give his interpretation, the way he saw things. Funny thing was nine out of ten times Dame would be right, he had learnt a lot from Dame. He remembered how parents on the side line would get a little carried away,

Grant in all his wisdom would go over to them, or if he was the referee he would stop the game head over to the parents give them a piece of his mind, sometimes most times, things didn't end well. After the game when Dame was alone with his dad he would explain why he thought Grant had it wrong how it could have been done without aggravation. Such wisdom from such a young age, this had been going on since Dame was around eight. Grant thought just like a boy yet he could discern situations so well.

The rowing days were good times. Grant has always been proud every time he would look down and see Dame rowing hard never giving in even though when Dame started to row he was the smallest in the crew, he made up for it in heart attitude (the boy he had stood down from the crew Dame had said to give him one more chance, had he listened things would have been different, three boys would still be alive!).

The times Dame had gone out of his way to befriend boys at college, who were not with in the crowd, Dame would build them up, walk beside them as they started to move in a new circle of friends. Then go find another boy. Dame never thought he was doing anything special it was just what he did. Then in would come the thoughts; Well that is all gone because of you, you never went with your son, you let the whole crew down, you let all the families down, had you gone none of this would of happened. This had a majorly detrimental effect on his future and the decisions he made. (If at any time in life negative thoughts overcome you laugh at them yes even though the laughter will have to be forced out. It will be a better outcome, less pain. (Try it and you will see for yourself)

Grant was awake…. wide awake. Tears began to flow down his face, he was consumed with guilt. This guilt was a lie straight from the pits of hell, put into Grant's mind at the time he believed it was his fault.

It was night time he thought at least I've had a few hours' sleep. Grant tossed and turned and tossed and turned for the rest of the night. As morning arose he began to pray Lord God I don't understand any of what has happened, all I know is Dame is with you, help Dame's mum, sister's, brother, grandparents all who love Dame all his family and friends comfort them all. Help me to be strong for my family. I don't know what to do, what to say, all I know is pain. Not only my pain the pain of our whole family. It hurts so much please help us to get through this time.

Grant looked toward Col as she lay there, he thought of all he had put her through. How good she was as a mother, wife, friend and was wondering how they were going to make it through this major hurdle. Was this going to be the end of their marriage? Maybe Col would realize everything was his fault. This was the battle that continued to rage on in Grant's mind.

It was time to get up Grant went out into the kitchen looked at what was on offer made a coffee sat down had a cigarette drank his coffee. Kelly and Nana soon came out sat down; followed by Col no one ate. Col's Sister, Mum and Kelly were heading home as there was really nothing more they could do here. Soon the time came when it was just Grant and Col. Grant rang the morgue to get a release time for Dame's body. Unfortunately the person he was talking to didn't have many people skills or compassion. He didn't give out anything, now you could say "Grant was under pressure he was only trying to get his son's body to take home." Grant was not happy or even slightly impressed by the answers or the attitude he was experiencing. So he told the person he was talking to he would be ringing back after lunch if no answers were given he would be down to pick up Dame's body look out if any one tried to stop him! This went down like a lead balloon. (It is important to remember when going through anything traumatic in life. The people you deal with 99 percent of time are awesome; sometimes however the other 1 percent they haven't got there.

This is not easy to deal with in hind sight try and remember. It is only a job to this 1 percent their attitude can be it is not my problem I'm doing my Job what's your problem?)

The rest of the morning seemed to take forever; he tried to keep himself busy. No matter how or what he tried to do his mind kept turning to Dame why his body had not been released. The people at the morgue where only doing their job, trying to get answers that may help another family in some way. Grant new deep inside to hand everything over to Jesus: He didn't; funny thing when we know we should turn left so we turn right, even though we know in our heart we should turn left, as it will be a better journey. Knowing it is very likely to be a rough journey carrying on as we are we keep going, heading straight for trouble. This is how Grant was felling he knew how he was feeling was wrong he not only felt stupid he was not helping anyone or anything good to happen.

Then it was lunch time he had been watching the clock ticking time to hurry up. Now lack of sleep after everything that had happened, he rang the morgue and was told they couldn't tell him when Dame's body would be released. Grant lost it and he could feel from deep inside something rising, sure enough out it came. The person on the other end of the phone had no idea what to say as he let him have it "if you haven't got my son's body ready to be picked up at 3pm to be put on a plane I will be down there and I will start with you". He was angry and they knew this at the mortuary.

As he sat trying to calm down all he wanted to do was take Dame's body home. They already knew what the cause of death was, they knew how, so why?

At that moment Grant's phone rang it was his best mate Stretch. "How you doing?" he asked" "Ok I guess "he replied "You can't go abusing and threatening people" Stretch said "I know all I won't is to bring Dame home" he replied. "Dame's body will be released at four pm to the undertaker who will take Dame's body to the airport to be put on the plane you all will fly home. "Stretch told Grant "Thank you" he felt relieved as he told Col of the new developments they were going home.

That afternoon a friend picked up Grant and Col. Her intention was to give them a couple of hours sightseeing. They ended up at their friend's house having a hot drink, passing time until their flight. Sometimes all you need is to be still in a quiet place and not really say or do much. Grant was thinking about all sorts of things not one thought took hold of his thoughts he was trying not to let any guilt, shame come into his mind he just wanted to grieve Dame's passing. As the travelled to the airport they never said much their thoughts were somewhere else. When Grant and Col arrived at the airport Air New Zealand looked after them with such care and compassion their transition onto the plane was effortless. As he sat on the plane his thoughts soon turned to Dame, what if I had gone away with the boys? Why had we moved from New Plymouth? Life is going to be different without Dame. Grant looked at Col and what he saw saddened his heart even more. There was brokenness a pain. Grant Pain was never ending and just when he thought the pain was at its greatest he would hurt like he had never hurt before. Thankfully Jesus was never more than a call away. How hard it must be for a mother. For the mother carries the child, then gives birth and every time Dame was unwell he would go straight past Grant to his mum, this is going to be a challenge a real trial. How am I going to look after my family when I'm such a mess myself? Grant thought.

Psa_94:14 For Jehovah will not leave His people; nor will He forsake His inheritance.

He wondered what Dame is doing now, if only I could have spoken to him and got a response! Would that have made any difference just being able to talk tell him how much he was loved Grant will never know. What he did know was how peaceful Dame looked when he parsed over no fear just peace. Throughout the flight, the hostesses would ask Grant and Col if they were ok and if there was anything they can get for them. Soon they were being told to fasten their seatbelts ready for landing. We are nearly home thought Grant.

As they walked down the corridor toward the terminal not much was said. A couple of days earlier, they had been going the other way in the same corridor toward the unknown now they were back with their son's body. The unknown had been revealed to him in a way he had never imagined or thought about. There were many things he had thought about like burying one of his children. Not that it would have made a lot of difference for there was nothing in his mind at that time could have prepared him for the passing of his son.

It is odd, the ones closest to us we hurt the most! It should not be this way the ones we love who are close should always be looked after and treated better than anyone even when we don't feel like it. No matter what is said or what is thought by others it is harder to love to give when we don't feel like it for whatever reason. (Try to look to the opposite especially in times of anger) he had many if only moments as reflected on the short time he had with Dame.

As Grant came through the doors there was Stretch waiting with his wife, what a good friend. Having major trials in his own life, yet hear he is looking after his friend putting his own feelings on hold. There he was helping his friend his time of need awesome. Grant thought "I'm going to always be there for him." If only Grant had but he never followed through with that thought.

They all arrived at the front doors of the airport. Grant wanted to ride in the hearse as it would be the last ride together Him and Dame. He wanted to be near his son's body for as long as possible even though he knew it was a body and Dames spirit was gone. The girls went off to go in stretches car Grant and Stretch waited at the front doors. What a good friend what a good man his friend was a real doer with a huge heart.

As he looked down the road leading up to the front door (there was a rise in the road so as you looked down the road cars approaching the front doors, the roof appeared first then the rest of the vehicle) he saw the hearse appearing maybe this was not such a good idea. He thought as he began to feel something, well up from deep in his heart. What got to Grant was the knowing that Dame's body sitting in that hearse, knowing that this was the last time they would ride together, knowing if he had lived more for his family this would not have happened as Dame would have been traveling with him. That guilt and condemnation will consume anyone, anytime with no discrimination. For if the door is left open even just a little then no matter how big how strong someone is; it comes in. This door way will be an area in life left undealt with it could be emotional it could be physical. Whatever area is not dealt with in life be sure to clean up your own back yard, anything from the past not dealt with properly. Even if not straight away don't be fooled for it just waits for the right time to manifest in a life.

Walking through grief especially family someone close, could make a person more likely to move towards negative thinking or actions.

Give it all to Jesus. He will help.

It seemed to take forever for the hearse to reach the front doors where they stood time seemed to slow down. Grant knew this wasn't going to be a pleasant trip and at some stage it was all going to become too much. Amongst all the grief sadness loss and every other emotion he was feeling. There was a peace. It was far away deep in his soul his inner self he didn't know why. Even when he was at a sad/low time he could feel a peace a love understanding. This did not mean he never found it hard sometimes he never knew what to do or how to cope, he just kept on going because that was all he was capable of at that time.

> *Joh 14:27 "Peace I leave with you, My peace I give to you. Not as the world gives do I give to you. Let not your heart be troubled, neither let it be afraid".*

Grant was afraid he was sad; it felt like he was in a sea instead of the front seat of the hearse.

There was a mist he couldn't swim or move it felt like he was being consumed and Grant had only been in the hearse five minutes. There was not a lot of talking in the journey to their home. The scenery went by without even being noticed; the time seemed to stand still. People getting on with their day, some happy some exited some sad all different emotions, none aware of the loss passing by them at that moment. As they travelled closer to their home a great sense of loss, began to overwhelm Grant. The guilt of not traveling with the boys grew in his mind.

Grant had driven this road so many times with Dame, he drifted off. He was on his way home from rugby laughing and joking! His mate in this moment Dame was sitting on the seat beside him. The mind is a powerful part of the body. Grant had to learn not to slip into a place of despair. Sometimes just to do normal everyday things became so hard whenever he let his mind wander.

Then they arrived. His dreaming was over; it was a nice day not too hot not raining. The hearse came to a stop.

So many people all to welcome Dame home for the last time. People of all ages, so many people joined together as one to welcome Dame home and say their goodbyes…..

Grant watched as the coffin was taken out the hearse, the pain is all consuming like nothing he had experienced. And all he could do was watch he wanted to rip the lid off grab Dame to tell him how much he loved him how much he was part of his life. How sorry he was he hadn't gone away with him! When the coffin makes its journey from the hearse to inside the house, sadness, grief, unbelief consumed everyone. Grant looked on a broken man feeling like part of himself was missing. Believing none of this pain sorrow would have been if he had not thought about himself so much, too late now he thought.

When he had made the choice to stay behind on this trip, he had just started a new job and did not want to put his employment at risk. Was it the right choice! Many times Grant had made decisions that had been wrong self-centred, now all those decisions seemed to come flooding back in his mind.

As Grant's eyes took in the scene before him, all the sadness, sorrow, broken hearted people, he held Col.

She was sobbing he was overcome with guilt what have I done was the thought that consumed him from that moment. It wasn't until many years later he understood, was able to let go of the guilt the shame the brokenness. This followed him wherever he went for many years, like a cloud consuming his every thought, move, action.

(Looking back he realizes how being so consumed with guilt was the doorway that held him in a place of absolute sorrow, guilt, depression, this turned to self-destruction.) Don't go there recognise any thought, feeling, action taken for what it is, for what the repercussions will be. One thing in life anyone can count on is the belief that whatever one sows, one reaps. Always try to see the good it is not easy it is worth it!

Dame's body was placed in the lounge to rest, be available to any who wanted to spend time and say their goodbyes. There Dame's body stayed for three days.

Chapter 4

Having Dame's body at home helped so many people in so many ways. A lot of people said why have the body at home?

Grant just knew it was the right thing to do. He just couldn't leave part of his family by them self's at any funeral home no matter how nice.

(This is not for everyone, and is not written to bring condemnation unrest to anyone) Over the days Dame's body lay at home, a healing took place. Not super spiritual or religious, more supernatural. There were no fancy prayers just a peace that seemed to consume the people young and old. The young people who had gathered, some had known Dame from a very young age, some through surf club, some from rugby, some from college, Dame's family, aunties, uncles, nieces, nephews all gathered spent time with Dame's body, said their goodbyes.

Grant watched all the time in his heart believing it was his fault; sometimes the guilt was so strong. That feeling everybody knows it's your fault, waiting for him to admit to put things right. Only he didn't know how to put things right, so for a long time it all stayed on his shoulders within himself. The torment went on for months in his mind. The Strange thing is in reality he did admit the whole thing was his fault. To no avail he got told not to be silly, of course it is not your fault. These comments were well….. Meaningless. Unfortunately they went straight over Grant. He just carried on trying to accommodate the guilt the shame in his life. In this time he decided no one understood so "I will keep how I'm feeling, so from now on no one will know how I feel". This was not the right way to deal with all that was going on in his life; no one knew the mess he was in major majorly hurting. On the outside it appeared he had everything worked out under control how wrong appearances can be.

While in this dark place there was a light that shone. Have you ever been driving in the country side and you see a light.

Now you know that light is far away, it looks so close, it looks so big and yet in reality it is probably a lone light. This is how life was for Grant in darkness but there is light if only I could get into the light…..

As he knew the light was Jesus, he would never leave him so why the darkness? Could it be the choices he had made had left Jesus waiting for his return? For The right choices and decisions will bring him back into the arms of Jesus. (This applies to anyone who desires peace. No matter where life is for you Jesus is waiting to walk with you into your future.)

The day before Dame was buried he had to be taken away as the makeup had been rubbed of his face. Even though Dame's body was returning to the house and even though he knew in his heart it was only his body, he knew the next time Dame's body left the house it would never return. This was something he had to work through everyone had to work through Col, Kelly it is very important to remember in any time of grief as much as you hurt there is usually someone hurting the same or more. Most often people will say they are fine when the truth is they are hurting like they've never hurt before. Whether not to burden anyone with the hurt they are feeling or maybe the pain in their life is unexplainable. Maybe they don't won't to appear weak, to be vulnerable whatever the reason listen to them and love them. Be there not giving advise not saying what your opinion is listening or maybe just being there will be enough. (if like Grant you have a hard time defining love look At 1 Corinthians 13 in the bible)

The first couple of nights there were tears lots and lots of tears as all different friends and family sat with Dame as his body lay in the living room holding his hand or rubbing Dame's forehead as they said their goodbyes. Early in the morning on first night Grant walked over to the casket looked down there lay His son his mate. Whoever was sitting beside Dame's body moved away as he sat down he looked at the lifeless body that was once so full of life an energy so contagious it would go before Dame falling on all around him. Now we'll all that was before him was a lifeless body his son's lifeless body. Grant really believed with all his heart Dame was in a better place.

Being beside Dame's body brought out emotions feelings from way down deep inside whoever else was in the room where time everything around him faded as he tried to deal with what was happening. After a time how long he wasn't sure he got up. It was a strange thing for him as he was overcome with a peace and yet the loss he was feeling, the guilt shame was never far away.

Dame's friends, family put different things in the coffin like gifts, notes, or memories some were things Dame liked doing like there was a new skateboard deck. Someone put a little miniature skateboard in the coffin, much to Dame's little brothers delight he had a great time playing with that little skateboard. It made things so much easier in a lot of ways having young children. The innocence lack of understanding is something to be thankful for in younger children. It can be like a breath of fresh air. You can hold them close giving them a hug helping in the release of healing, the child be hugged has no idea usually happy to receive the attention/love. Many times they would ask the questions that for whatever reason adults or teenagers didn't ask. This meant Grant faced some things in a more direct way.

If some things asked by Dame's younger brother and sister had been asked by anyone else the answer would have been different, the reaction would have been different. Only because if we have a choice we tend to leave some things until later to deal with, and they get left undealt with. This is not a good way to deal with issues that arise, it can turn little issues into mountains, that get left undealt with so causing anxiety and pain every time they resurface. Maybe because in answering certain questions we have to face something we are not ready to answer or face. That's ok just don't let the question go unanswered for ever. Write it down put it away for later (don't forget about it DEAL WITH IT) then work through the question, area when the time is right.

On the last night something changed there were a lot of Dames mate's boys, girls young not so young in fact as Grant stood at the door he wondered how they all fitted in the room. It was the last night, the last time he would be able to look into the room and see Dame's body. Even though he believed Dame was in a better place it was a hard time.

Grant was finding it difficult on one hand he knew in his heart Dame was in a better place on the other hand he missed Dame so much, and all he saw in front of him was a lifeless body. In such times of confusion he grew to rely on Jesus.

The guilt the shame raised its ugly head again consuming him. So he did what he was good at made it look like he was in control, when the truth was he was falling apart from the inside out. Still he tried to look after be there for his wife and eldest daughter who were going through their own trials what do you do? Be there when they need you when they fall put your arm out to help them up give to them what they need he found this was this was usually opposite to what he thought. Grant had to learn not to rely on what his thoughts / feelings where to think look deep inside wait before he spoke. This did not come naturally to him. Again being there sometimes was all that is needed, to hold close maybe tears or just sitting saying nothing everyone every situation different. Be there for those who need you!

Grant noticed the change in atmosphere everyone was more relaxed, there was singing stories of times spent together with Dame, laughing a joy filled not only the room but the whole house.

> *Rom 15:13 "And may the God of hope fill you with all joy and peace in believing, that you may abound in hope through the power of the Holy Spirit".*

As the night went on a great peace fell over all in the house. Peace fell on everybody no matter what they believed. God loves us all no matter how good or what we have done or were we have been, Grant was in ore he felt a freedom. All the pain, guilt, loss, sorrow was taken away in its place was a love so Glorious. The morning came a little too fast for him, for he knew the time was drawing near when the lid would be placed on the coffin. Grant wanted to stay in the peace, love that was the presence of the highest Lord God Jehovah. As time passed he understood God is God and there is a freedom like no other in knowing Jesus. (Look in the back of this book if you want the freedom, peace love that is Jesus) Although he believed that Dame was in heaven, it was one of those times that he felt like his heart was being pulled out all the pain returned, and yet there was an underlying peace. In times of trial we must learn to captivate our thoughts to think about what we are thinking about. (There are many good teachings on how to do and live this way) As a Dad he needed to know Dame was safe so the peace he felt amongst all the pain turmoil going on in his life there was knowing from deep inside Dame was safe still he looked for confirmation. Grant thought about God why had he let this accident happen why did three young lives' get cut short? (It is a sad fact when tragedy comes God gets the blame Grant never blamed God it took a while to understand why. Please don't put your head in the sand and say there is no adversary, only God, not Satan. That is like being in a battle with the enemy inflicting great loss to the army before you and saying I'm not in a battle) The why question is the same question he had asked and asked then asked again. The only answer he ever seemed to get was a peace a knowing Dame was ok.

Grant needed more' it was awesome having the peace the knowing still he felt raw pain emptiness, like something was missing. Then whenever there was a chance the guilt the shame returned overcoming him. (Because he let it knowing no better at the time)

Grant kept going back, they were standing outside the undertakers waiting to see Dame's body as they were dressing and preparing Dame's body. Col turned to Grant and said "I really believe Damion is in heaven" from that moment when doubt or unbelief tried to raise its ugly head he was taken back to that moment. Why? Col was not a believer she had seen Grant go up and down, be strong, be weak, which didn't help in her salvation, so when she said "Damion was in heaven" with such conviction something moved in his spirit in his heart his soul "Confirmation" Dame was ok.

As he looked down on Dame's body lying so still so peaceful he felt a tap on his shoulder it was time to put the lid on! The lid only needed a few screws as the lid would be taken off for Dame's service. The lid being placed on the coffin, wow he broke.

It seemed as though he was back in the hospital being told Dame wasn't going to make it, he trembled from the inside out. Everything was a blur he was never going to see Dame's face hear his voice again on earth. This time is not easy no matter how strong, how much pain one can handle. He started to think of every time he had let Dame down, overreacted, stood his ground not wanting his son to grow up the wrong way. Why?

Again and Again he asked himself why? He knew in his heart he had not been a bad dad maybe a bit stubborn, unrelenting strict to overbearing all he wanted was Dame not to grow up doing the same having the same issues as his dad! Grant wants anyone who is has or is going through this time to know Jesus is there with you, and in time you learn to live with your loss. You never forget you learn to live with your loss. You gain more compassion, more empathy towards people who have suffered. Please don't let your loss go inward. By this he means try not to become bitter angry as this will only bring more pain and suffering on yourself and those you love. Cry out to Jesus no not in some religious way. From your heart he is there waiting for you to help you. He will wrap his arms of love around you.

In all he believes through all the trials good and not so good Jesus was there. Many times he made the wrong decision went down the wrong road, when he could go no further, he would turn around there waiting with his arms open Jesus waited. Try getting to know Jesus for who he is not with anyone else's view point open up to make friends with Him there is a pleasant surprise waiting!

All too soon it was time as he left the house he knew this part of the journey was drawing to an end. As the car approached the church people so many people the building was not big. There was only room for about a hundred people the rest had to be outside, and there were plenty, all these people have come to say goodbye to pay their last respects. As a father he felt proud in a good way for a moment in time, all the guilt all the pain all the grief took a backseat. As the car drove into the car park it was like a sea of people, parting to let the car in flowing back in behind it. The car stopped it was time to get out! Strange have you ever been somewhere and yet it is like you're not there?

Grant felt exactly that feeling as he and his family walked into the building. Maybe he knew the end was near it had been a long week, the longest week in his life. The service got under way Grant could not remember much he was there but not there maybe he was being spared the added grief? As they left the service walking behind the coffin the song I will always love you playing the sadness in people's eyes, the song, maybe the realisation the end was near he was never going to be able to talk hold hear Damion's voice, he broke tears that were in his eyes began flowing like a undammed river he felt weak the next thing he knew they were traveling in a vehicle heading towards the beach.

Because of Dame's love of the beach the local surf lifesaving club, his mates and fellow clubbies asked what Grant and Col thought of Dame's last ride being in a surf boat with his surf board placed near his coffin. After the service Dame's last journey (his body) would be along the beach before heading to the cemetery. As the convoy followed behind they all headed to the cemetery. No one should have to bury a child; and yet every day somewhere in the world exactly this happens daily.

No matter where this happens or when it is never an easy time to go through. In the western part of the world we can watch or see devastation and yet it is like we become conditioned. This is sad as the loss to every mother, father, brother, sister husband, or wife really makes little difference and it still hurts. The damage can be wide spread, affecting not only the immediate family. Friends are often overlooked in times of grief, a good friend can be as close as family. Grant realized some of Dame's friends where close. His death had a major impact on their lives. As hard as it was at the time Grant and Col opened their home their heart to the ones who felt and where close to *Dame. It was a hard thing to do as in a time of grief of loss the last thing he felt like doing was listening to complete strangers talk about how close the where to of his son. Really, how come Dame never mentioned these people he would never have known about the relationship Dame had with these people had he not taken the time out to listen to try and help them through their pain. Every time he did this a healing occurred in his own life or in his family's life.*

Dame's coffin was carried to its place of final resting by Grant family friends this can be a hard decision to make who carries the coffin all they could do was try and accommodate everyone, this is not an easy decision. The last words were spoken as the coffin entered the grave this was a reality check for in his heart he knew the body of Dame was gone. It is a strange place to be in, accepting Dame was gone. And yet he could look upon his body, even though he knew Dame had gone from the body he still found comfort just being able to see his body. Now that body was getting lowered into the ground the final step on this part of the journey.

One man on guitar began to sing the songs turned to worship. Suddenly he needed to bury his son, cover the casket with dirt. There were shovels not far away after checking with the sexton (caretaker of the cemetery) while they sang a few men together with Grant buried Dame's coffin. When they had finished Grant stuck his shovel in the dirt mounded up on top of the grave and said "it is finished".

Chapter 5

That part of the journey was finished, after the burial everyone went back to have food and drink this was pleasant as it could be under the circumstances, this was after all the third funeral in four days. Funny thing was for years he had been able to get away from reality drinking alcohol this night he felt different. He had been one of the people who stayed till the end drank everything and really was thinking well usually nothing other than how he could enjoy himself. This night was different instead of being part of the culture, after a while he sat by himself with his thoughts. Listening to the ones drinking getting louder and louder instead of guilt or sadness, sorrow or pain, anger began to grow from deep down then like an explosion came out half an hour later while he was on his way home. When he walked in the door the house was quiet. The first door he came to was the boy's room. As he looked in the room, he saw there fast asleep, his son Jake. His gaze moved and he saw the empty bed where Dame slept.

He was gone never to return he was filled with sorrow and yet at the same time peace a knowing Dame was safe. He went to bed trying to get some sleep what a day, unsure how what the future held.

It seemed for a while people gave him more leniency with regard to his actions, as time was needed for healing. Whether not enough space time was allowed, or maybe because he had a lot more to learn surrender, a lot more damage was to be done. Unfortunately this damage was done to those closest to him. Although at the time he could not see what toll this was having on those close to him. It was as though on one hand he was doing all he could to help protect those he loved, on the other hand he was in a self-destruct mode and this is not a good place to be in. Although he knew what he was doing is not right try as he did in his own strength he could not stop. In his mind he had been hurt and come through now most everything he did was wrong so subconsciously he put up a huge wall that helped him cope. He did try any little thing but it was not going as he thought it should set him off.

Time keeps going forward however for some people trying to move on with their lives. This time can be as hard as going through the original trauma. Well-meaning friends and family can say things meant to comfort help all concerned to get through it doesn't. Grant learnt a valuable lesson one of many. Never say "I understand" to anyone if he had never walked through (been in the same situation). Even if the motive for doing so is to help for good, it does a lot more just to be there. This may seem harsh you may even be thinking well I know my best friend passed on or a good friend of mine, went through a tragic time in their life, so I understand. Grant thought the same until Dames untimely passing. There is a huge difference between when your life is turned upside-down, than having known someone who's life has been turned upside-down just being there for someone when your angry, just being there when your sad, just being there when your broken, just being there. Not giving advice or telling you it will be ok in time, you really have to move on! These are a couple things said to him that at the time didn't help. Yes time eases the pain and yes in a way life moves on. Time never means you forget if you want the memory to be with you good memory's. The choice is in the hands of everyone who has experienced loss.

At the time spoken it was not what he wanted to hear (even though it was truth) it was not what he wanted to hear or needed to hear. In time he did move on, it took a lot of time and much heartache, real soul searching to do this.(If there is someone close going through a trial be there let them know you don't understand what they are going through, listen be there so they know your there) Yes as a father he had three other children, that needed him, he had a wife that had walked this journey with him, and was broken, still functioning well, looking after the children and being there for them, still broken on the inside. Maybe he tried too hard to help others and forgot about himself in doing so could only help others so much before it would become too much and like a ticking time bomb he would explode. Not always did he explode outwardly sometimes imploding, the imploding ended up causing more trouble and pain as it would eventually come out not good result for anyone concerned!

Some things remind us of a person we've lost from our life where Grant and Col lived was on a hill, buses would go up the road, below their house all day and half the night. In the afternoon around three forty five a college bus would go up the hill. Col would here that bus every day and be waiting for Dame to walk in the back door. This meant every week day she would relive this moment over and over. The only way to resolve this was to move to sell the house. Sometimes changing the surroundings is enough to bring change. Not to forget to move on start healing accepting deep within what has taken place. Grant was back at work functioning on the outside it looked like life was returning to some sort of normality. Appearances can be deceiving even to the person involved soon enough cracks started to appear. Unfortunately for him no one saw anything wrong so on he went playing life like a game of charades. All the while down deep inside like a volcano getting ready to erupt. He had no idea what he was feeling within himself would eventually come out in ways that would even leave him confused and dismayed.

Maybe helping others will help you not to become bitter as this tends to make things worse in every area of your life. Try to keep focused on things that are right things that help others. Grant struggled on for a long time never finding someone who understood. Maybe he never looked hard enough maybe he wasn't ready to open up to trust, to let go.

He had never really dealt with Dames passing put other way the pressure had not been released. It didn't have to be this way had he known how to surrender all to Jesus instead of surrendering ninety or even ninety nine percent, things would have been different. Surrendering is not an easy thing to do often he knew the choice he made was wrong the consequences were going to be far reaching. And still the choice would be made, usually leaving him more confused in more pain longing for a better way a smoother road to travel.

There are many areas different emotions that seem to just arrive before you know it you are doing strange things acting in odd ways. As it had not been a long time since the burial of Dame and his emotions where all over the place.

Grant never set out to hurt anyone and yet he would say and do things that would hurt. Looking back he realizes the untimely passing of Dame had rocked his world more than he had realized.

Grant never blamed God never even thought it was Gods fault. And yet many people could not understand this. Someone has to be to blame mostly this is God why? Maybe it's easier to put the blame Gods way! There is hardly ever any mention of satin the devil is this because if satin is blamed then God must be real? Sometimes it is easy if the belief things happen is easier to deal with. Whatever is decided try not to be fooled into a false sense of peace? The thoughts that come into a mind don't just fall on in there; they are for good or evil. Try and look think about every thought that enters into your mind. This may not always be easy as some thoughts we try to justify. Try using this measure if this thought/action doesn't edify help someone cast it out think opposite do the opposite even when it is the last thing we might feel like doing, do it then release will come. If nothing changes the first time don't give up keep on doing what is right for others.

This did not come naturally for Grant and it took time. When the guilt, shame, pain, loss would find its way back into his life he would try and focus on other's needs. It may be the person with a need is someone you have trouble helping. Grant found focusing on their need helped him overcome some dark times when there seemed to be no light at the end of the tunnel. Try as he did to think of others for a time he would accomplish all he set out to do. However he never seemed to get very far by himself he called out to Jesus many times and every time it became easier. Grant wants to make clear he was not someone who lived a life of a Christian in fact you could say he lived the opposite. However he is thankful through Jesus, Lord God Jehovah poured out mercy and grace on him.

His life did carry on not as normal there were issues hidden too painful to deal with in his own strength. Over time he learnt to deal with many areas he had hidden deep within himself. Like so many others he didn't know how to bring release from the torment in his life the unrelenting torment.

He did go back to smoking drugs, drinking not realising he was slipping faster and further into darkness than he had ever been before. Against everything he knew had been taught about Jesus about God he knew in his heart he was not alone. Jesus was waiting for him to realize the path he'd chosen was a dead end to turn back to him. To do what you know is wrong to know the result is going to be more pain, and yet Grant found he was in that exact place not fun or good place to be in. The strange thing was he wanted to be a better person to cast of every stigma associated to him, let go of the past start afresh. Yet he was going down some of the same paths only he seemed to be going harder deeper into darkness. Why he couldn't understand then as God says he will use the foolish things of the world to confound the wise.

1Co 1:27 "But God has chosen the foolish things of the world to confound the wise; and God has chosen the weak things of the world to confound the things which are mighty"

He is learning a new way of living of thinking always remember God is a loving Father who's plan for your life is not grief, pain or regret.

Jesus paid an awesome price for your salvation one that if realized will set you free in a way like no other.

Grant hopes you will understand, when he mentions Jesus it has nothing to do with any man made religion. He has and continues to build an intimate friendship like no other he has ever known. The overwhelming peace strength this has given him in all sorts of situations has given him the ability to move on to go forward with his life. He doesn't get it right all the time in fact sometimes he has made a real mess of things made the completely wrong decision/choice. After he has had his very own pity party thinking he's blown it why would anyone let alone Jesus/God won't anything to do with him? He feels a love so pure so unconditional it consumed him. Thank you Jesus.

The result of Grant's choices is another story in his journey.

Chapter 6

In this story Grant has quoted scripture, in this chapter Grant will do his best to explain what they meant to him at the time. How God helped him through what seemed like a tunnel with no end. Grant is not a theologian, he has not attended a bible college nor had any teaching other than experience. It is not Grant's intention to offend anyone the explanation given applies to his life and what he was going through. If it helps you awesome one thing Grant has learnt is we all have a choice!

What, how why, How to1Co_1:27 "But God hath chosen the foolish things of the world to confound the wise; and God hath chosen the weak things of the world to confound the things which are mighty"

When Grant came to know Jesus he was truly one who did many foolish things, at the time he thought they were clever or cool. His concept of Jesus and God, was something far and untouchable. Why would they want anything to do with me?

This was Grant's thinking at that time. His decisions on what he should do or say, most of the time we're weak. This left many people scratching their head, why? Can someone who has no regard for others, someone who seems to make stupid decisions, a fool through and through. Yet he always seems to get through. Uninjured physically it was like an angel helped Grant (he was so thankful many times he wondered after he heard what he had done and said he wondered why? This was right down to the way he thought, knowing what he was doing, thinking and saying was wrong silly foolish. Yet he kept on being foolish. Leaving people scratching their heads in wonder as to how this can be. Grant still had a way to go, to grow in fact in his own words he had taken the first step.....

> *2Peter 2:22: "A dog goes back to its vomit," and "A sow*
> *that has been washed goes back to roll around in the mud".*

Anyone walking through, had any major trial in their life (Remember a major trial for one may be nothing to another) may see their past clearly.

Such as things being done, attitudes all different areas of life become clear for what the consequence to not only self also many others including family. This happened to Grant and he thought "I'm never going to that again! He never wanted to go back to his old ways, and yet he did. His journey back all started with a thought.

However before long he found some old habits returned only now they seemed worse.

> *Mat 12:43-45 "When the unclean spirit has gone out of*
> *a man, he walks through dry places seeking rest, and finds*
> *none. Then he said, I will return into my house from where*
> *I came out. And when he has come, he finds it empty, swept,*
> *and decorated. Then he goes and takes with him seven other*
> *spirits more evil than himself, and they enter in and live*
> *there. And the last state of that man is worse than the first.*
> *Even so it also shall be to this evil generation".*

Grant had no understanding about cleaning out his house (body) then leaving the house cleaned out tidy but empty. He heard many years later about empty space being a place. And the penny dropped, he found Jesus seen the mess his life was and decided to try putting it in order.

He had not realized (understood) that as he became clean (free) from all sorts of things he was not filling the part of himself cleaned out so empty it stayed. Now he knows to fill everything with the word of God, being pacific. For instance if anger is cast out ask for peace to fill the place vacated finding scriptures on peace speaking them out confessing them to the clean place made vacant by anger leaving.

Maybe it was the pain, the frustration, the sense of guilt, or was it because he didn't know; all he had to do was get closer to Jesus. If this is where or somewhere close to a place anyone can relate to call out to Jesus. Don't wait just do it, get to know him. In Grant's life one thing he cannot say is he never had love in his life. The unconditional love, acceptance from Jesus he had never known. IT was not like there was any condemnation it was more like this is where you are Do you want to be free of this? Remember we all have choices.

Rom 7:19 "For the good which I have a mind to do, I do not: but the evil which I have no mind to do, that I do"

So when he found himself back doing things he didn't want to be doing, this caused confusion on ("Why do I keep doing these things"?) This would just cause more low self-esteem to overtake him yet he knew deep in his heart what had to be done to move out of this place he seemed to be in!

Grant knew he was doing wrong! He didn't want to keep doing the same things he was doing so he started to learn how to change. As all he was doing was holding off the inevitable unless he learnt, so he embarked on the journey of change: On his journey he fell many times and to this day continues to fall. The major difference is now he knows to get up quickly look forward not back and give everything to Jesus.

1Sa 22:23 "Keep here with me and have no fear; for he who has designs on my life has designs on yours: but with me you will be safe."

While Grant's Life was not in a good place everything he was doing whether right or wrong seemed to have no fear. There were things that brought shivers and fear tried hard to take hold. He knew all he had to do was trust in Jesus, this is easy to say but not so easy to do.

The time he nearly went off the road in the truck was one time he knew he was being watched over. Why he had no idea at the time all he knew he would be safe. The same sense of safety was with Grant throughout the passing of Dame even though some of the choices he made were all in all wrong. And there were times when he was lost so lost not knowing if he should turn right left or go straight ahead. There was always a sense of peace safety of a love so strong all consuming. He is not saying do whatever you want how you want and it's all good Jesus loves you it's all good no that is not the experience he had at all. He always tried to do what was right his desire was to be closer to Jesus so he learnt to spend time with him. In his Journey he just made some real bad choices, he doesn't know why he always felt safe. Could it have been because when Dame passed Grant confesses he was broken to a point he had no idea what to do or how to get there. Jesus seemed to know so he tried the best he could to follow him and in doing so he felt safe and as Grant let go fear became an emotion of the past.

Rom 7:19 "For the good which I have a mind to do, I do not: but the evil which I have no mind to do, that I do".

Drinking back in the old days and living a double life still hurts those he loved. He would have loved to do the right thing all the time, not good and then evil. This was not a fun place to be. Yet through this time in his life Rom 7:19 kept coming to his mind. He would find himself thinking about what he was doing and how he could do more good and less evil. How do I change? Oh how Grant wanted to change if only he knew how!

Then he realized it was his choice. Sounds easy enough he thought from now on the choices made will be the right ones. If only it had been as easy as that! So he did all he knew. He turned to Jesus for help, for guidance and over time is learning. There's so much more than he ever knew or thought or had been taught. Get to know Jesus.

Gal 6:7 "Do not be deceived, God is not mocked. For whatever a man sows, that he also will reap."

Prov 22:8 "He who sows iniquity shall reap vanity; and the rod of his anger shall fail."

The emotion Grant was feeling was like riding a rollercoaster. Try as he would he would be up doing good caring for all around him, and then within a moment in time he was back doing things his way. This usually involved selfishness, drinking, smoking and drugs. He could never understand why people around him would get so upset, why everything he would do never turned out well. It was never anything he did nor said! (so he thought) Again it was when Grant had destroyed almost all that was dear to him he realized the error of his ways through the choices he made. It was not like Grant was mocking God on purpose he definitely was in deception. Years of sowing was building up, like a dam building up getting ready to burst. He was starting to reap what he had sown not realising he was reaping seed he had sown already. If he had realized all he had to do was turn from his wicked selfish ways, do what is right the outcome of his life would have been a lot different.

Act 3:19 "Therefore repent and convert so that your sins may be blotted out, when the times of refreshing shall come from the presence of the Lord."

This verse is really easy self-explanatory well Grant thought so however try as he would repenting over and over trying not do the same things the same way. This he would be able to do for a short time a week even two or three weeks, only thing was it was being done in his own strength. Well mostly his own strength he was experiencing refreshing even knowing the presence. Though now Grant believes what he experienced was enough to get him through. Every time he repented and began to walk the right way it wouldn't be long before he looked back, then went back to his old ways. Why when all going back did was bring pain to himself and those he loved and near to him. So he would cry out to Jesus it was like Jesus was waiting with his arms outstretched. Grant has acknowledged many times how blessed he has been for if it was him doing the waiting he would have gotten tired and left! *2Ti 3:2-4 "For men will be self-lovers, money- lovers, boasters, proud, blasphemers, disobedient to parents, unthankful, unholy, without natural affection, unyielding, false accusers, without self- control, savage, despisers of good, traitors, reckless, puffed up, lovers of pleasure rather than lovers of God".*

At this time in Grant's life everything he did seemed to end up in a mess. He would be without self-control unable it would seem to control his mouth and what come out his mouth. He was out of control thinking only of self and nothing else. This seemed to be a recurring pattern in Grant's life, still every word out of scripture seemed to give him understanding of what needed to be done, where he was in that particular time in his life. He never felt any condemnation only a love so pure. And yet he kept making the wrong choices turning left instead of right. Even though outwardly he was out of control, inwardly he hurt for he wanted desired to be a better person, better husband, better father, better friend, and a better son. He was deceived into believing no matter what he did he was never going to change this was a lie put into his mind, so he carried on doing the things bringing devastation into his life!

> *Mar 4:40 "And He said to them, Why are you so fearful? How is it that you have no faith"?*

> *Joh 11:40 "Jesus answered her, Did I not say to you that if you would believe you would see the glory of God?"*

This part of God's word again it became alive to Grant again hopes it comes alive for you…….Although it took a while and there were times fear nearly had victory. Grant knew he had faith, he believed so he should have no fear. Thank you Jesus! Along came John 11:40. This verse gave Grant hope for he knew he needed to be in the glory and so began another awesome journey. This helped him to focus on something other than the loss of Dame. The best place to be is in the presence of Jesus maybe if he stuck close to Jesus he would find the glory!

> *Mat 22:37-40 "Jesus said to him, You shall love the Lord your God with all your heart, and with all your soul, and with all your mind. This is the first and great commandment. And the second is like it, You shall love your neighbour as yourself. On these two commandments hang all the Law and the Prophets".*

Grant was given a revelation he was reading the word on the Bible when this part of the word became alive. Grant realized he needed to love The Lord God Jehovah and his neighbour.

Whatever trial Grant faced, this scripture seemed to always end up being part of his focus, usually bringing him peace. This meant every circumstance of Dame's passing, the car crash, the people who had been involved and done, things acted in a way Grant had reacted, sometimes in the wrong way. He had loved as God loved him! As much as Grant would like to say he accomplished this he didn't always succeed. He never gave up even when things looked impossible. If he had an easy way tell you, if you do this or if you do that, there is no easy way only believe 1John 5:4-6. There began another awesome journey:

> *Psalm 20:6 "Now I know that Jehovah saves His anointed; He will hear him from His holy Heaven with the saving strengths of His right hand".*

As Grant tried to get through the passing of his son it felt surreal not happening to him his family, the peace given to him through this word, reinforced Dame was safe. There was a strength that kept him going.

When all Grant wonted was to wake up and find all that had happened was a dream! Although he still had lots of choices to make, and yes he made some wrong choices as time went on. At that time in the place it helped to know God loved him so much even with all his weaknesses and faults. This is life changing if you let it be want it to be. Don't listen when you hear Jesus is not real or you must do this or do that. All Grant did was call out to Jesus no wonderful payer no amassing experience or religious ceremony he called out with all he had within him. Turn to Jesus he is real and wants to be your friend, he will be a friend like no other try getting to know him. No matter what you have done or where you have been.

> *2Co 12:9 "And He said to me, My grace is sufficient for you, for My power is made perfect in weakness. Most gladly therefore I will rather glory in my weaknesses, that the power of Christ may overshadow me."*

> *Joh 14:27 "Peace I leave with you, My peace I give to you. Not as the world gives do I give to you. Let not your heart be troubled, neither let it be afraid".*

When you are in a place as, nothing seems to take the pain the confusion away. No matter how or what you try how or what we may do, to know there is someone who gives grace and mercy to help whoever wants it. There are times in our life (some more than others) when one thinks how am I going to get through this?

Grant was in this place completely lost. One thing that happened to Grant there seemed to be more thoughts about what he had done in his past thoughts that seemed to add more substance, none of this would have happened if he had made better choices.

This scripture came amongst one such time stopping the torment in Grant's life as in front of him sat a women who had been broken. Her life had been completely turned upside down not once, not twice, but three times, and yet there was peace and joy that emanated from her. Helping him to realize how it wasn't helping him or his family to focus on the negative. To live and be able to function was all he needed to do, without the masks. Strange how everything can look good on the outside when really our world is imploding and cracks start to appear.

These scriptures gave Grant peace, strength every time he needed peace and strength of which there were many.

*Psa_94:14 For Jehovah will not leave His people; nor will
He forsake His inheritance.*

Sometimes we need to know we are not alone, when no light can
be seen at the end of the tunnel. No matter where we are, how we
are feeling, Jehovah loves us and will not leave you alone. Even when
things are not how we think they should be Grant could always sense
the presence of Jesus. Grant would be feeling like everything going on
in his life was becoming too much. It was like he was standing on the
edge of a mighty canyon ready to fall.

However there were arms holding him peace filling him that was
just there helping him guiding him and his family through a very hard
time. Why? There is nothing special about Grant in fact he needed to
work on many things in his life!

*Joh 14:27 "Peace I leave with you, My peace I give to you.
Not as the world gives do I give to you. Let not your heart
be troubled, neither let it be afraid."*

Peace came to Grant every time this scripture came to mind. In
himself it was undeserved still but as soon as this scripture came to mind,
peace filled him. Whether he was feeling anxious, sad, alone, depressed
however he felt, peace would consume every part of Grant. This may
not always be instant and it may start deep within and consume him.
So even when things around him were chaotic, he had peace. There
were no conditions given to Grant he would get the thought and
realize it was scripture. He start believing and peace would come. It
was awesome, beautiful. So refreshing in turbulent times when every
part of Grant felt broken.

*Rom 15:13 "And may the God of hope fill you with all
joy and peace in believing, that you may abound in hope
through the power of the Holy Spirit."*

As the time came closer people knew Dame all he was all he stood for would be gone. To Grant his son was already gone moved on to be with Jesus. This helped knowing Dame was in a better place, still there where emotions, feelings all the fleshly side the reality his son was gone from his life. Then the night before the funeral as he stood in the doorway, he noticed a change in the atmosphere in everyone in the room. How can this be Grant thought then Rom 15: 13 began to consume his thoughts? This again helped his family all who were gathered, to get through. Be able to move on to the funeral where the final goodbyes were spoken. Amongst the grief, to be able to experience a change a shift a release from the loss of a friend a son, grandson, cousin. Remembering a lot of the people there had been through two funerals already. What happened in Grant's home is available to all who cry out to Jesus: for the joy the peace that comes from the throne of the highest Lord God Jehovah is beyond anything this world has to offer.

> *1Co_1:27 "But God hath chosen the foolish things of the world to confound the wise; and God hath chosen the weak things of the world to confound the things which are mighty".*

Chapter 7

e have a choice; choose where there is good fruit (things happen in life that are good unexplainable things) There are many different beliefs in the world Grant's thinking is in his time of need there was only Jesus who helped him through. He can only go on the evidence he experienced and continues to experience.

There is a place in Grant's heart that will always belong to Dame. Grant has learned overtime to live with Dame's passing. He will never forget Dame. He has accepted his passing and gets on with life. He has always told all his children he loves them the same. This helped him to realize their need in this journey and try to take into account their needs. Many times when everything was becoming too much, he would find himself with another of his children holding them, talking to them, listening to them this was a big part of his healing process.

The most important life changing moment of this whole journey was meeting Jesus not in a religious way.

There is so much more to Jesus than is often told/shown this is tragic and a lot of people miss out, never to know the freedom love and everything else available to all who seek him. As Grant has said "try calling to Jesus" when he called it wasn't because someone told him to, it was because he had come to the end of the road. Nothing else helped him through the pain he felt, Jesus has become his friend his best mate. Yes there are still a lot of areas he is working on in all things condemnation has gone replaced with a freedom, love that is so awesome and is available to all who seek after who God is who build an intimate relationship with God, who want to walk with Jesus.

Here is a way to call out to Jesus a way to ask him into your life say these words out loud! *"Jesus come into my life I surrender everything in me and about me to you."* Jesus loves you he wants to dwell with you, it is Grant's hope is life will take on a whole new meaning and you to will walk in fullness, freedom that is in Jesus.

Blessings and favour to you and your family!

THE Loss OF A SON

GRANT CROSS

Share this book if you feel that
this can inspire other people.

You can make a comment about
this book through Amazon.com

You can make use of the following
pages for you to remember
all your blessings in life.

9 798891 940031